OTHER CREEPIES FOR YOU TO ENJOY ARE:
The Flat Man
The Ankle Grabber
Jumble Joan

For Tom, Molly, and Alice (RI)
For Andrew (MK)

Text © 1988 Rose Impey
Illustrations © 1988 Moira Kemp
This edition designed by Douglas Martin.

This edition published in the United States of America in 2004 by
Gingham Dog Press
an imprint of School Specialty Children's Publishing,
a member of the School Specialty Family
8720 Orion Place, 2nd Floor, Columbus, OH 43240-2111

www.ChildrensSpecialty.com

Library of Congress Cataloging-in-Publication Data is on file with the publisher

This edition first published in the UK in 2003 by Mathew Price Limited.

ISBN 0-7696-3366-8
Printed in China.

1 2 3 4 5 6 7 8 9 10 MP 08 07 06 05 04

Scare Yourself to Sleep

By Rose Impey
Illustrated by Moira Kemp

GINGHAM DOG
P R E S S

Columbus, Ohio

My cousin has come to visit,
and tonight, we are sleeping
in a tent in the backyard.
We don't let my brother, Simon,
in the tent. He would spoil everything.

My cousin and I love that it is
just the two of us lying here,
side by side, talking.

We quietly tell each other jokes.
We don't want anyone
to know we're in here.

We know Simon is
outside the tent
trying to listen,
so we whisper.
We don't want him
to spoil everything.

Soon, it starts to get dark.
The shadows rise.
Outside, it grows
quiet and still.
Now, my cousin and I
play the game we always play.
We call it, "Scare Yourself to Sleep."

First, I whisper to her,
"Are you scared?"
"No," she says. "Are you?"
"No, but I bet I can scare you," I say.
"Go ahead and try," she says.
"All right, but remember, you asked for it."
Then, I begin to tell her all about
the Garbage Can Goblins.

They are the
evil little goblins that
live beneath the trash
at the bottom
of garbage cans.

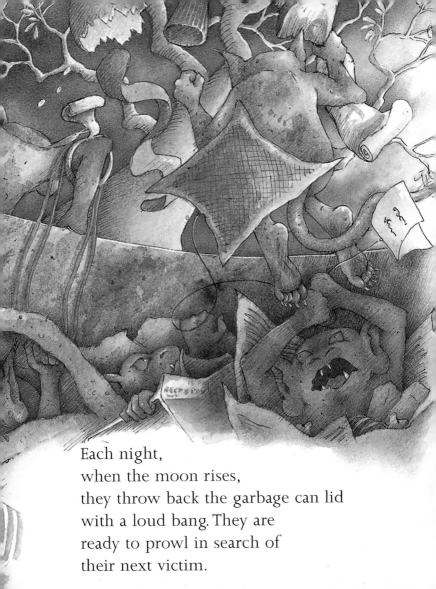

Each night,
when the moon rises,
they throw back the garbage can lid
with a loud bang. They are
ready to prowl in search of
their next victim.

The Garbage Can Goblins
fling all the rotten food
into the air.
Then, they crawl out,
climbing over one another
in their struggle to get free.
They swarm around the yard
until they find
some helpless creature that is
foolish enough to be out alone.

Then, they carry it,
struggling and squealing,
back to their smelly den,
never to be seen again.

My cousin is very quiet.
She wriggles down
into her sleeping bag.
I smile to myself.
I know I have scared her.

Suddenly, there is a loud
CRASH!
It sounds like a garbage can lid
banging in the yard.
We look at each other.
Our hearts are thumping.

Then, we hear, "Gotcha! Hee, hee, hee."

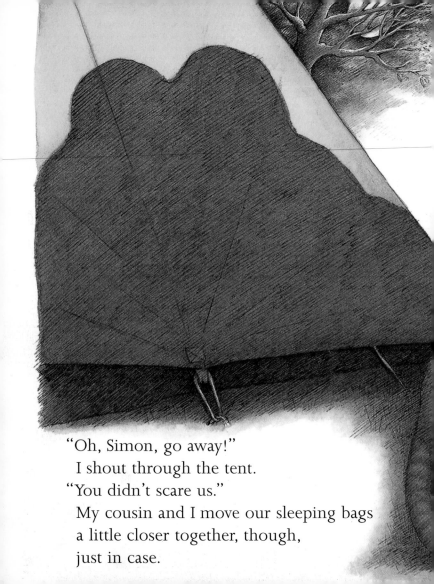

"Oh, Simon, go away!"
I shout through the tent.
"You didn't scare us."
My cousin and I move our sleeping bags
a little closer together, though,
just in case.

Now, my cousin tells me
about the Flying Cat.
It creeps along
on its soft, padded paws,
pretending to be
an ordinary cat.
When the clock strikes
midnight, it sprouts
wings and soars
into the air, like
a giant, furry moth.

"Never sleep with your tent open,"
   my cousin warns me.
"When the Flying Cat
   finds its prey, it swoops down
   to capture it."

"The Flying Cat sinks its claws
and its razor-sharp teeth
into its victim.
It sucks its blood.
Slurp, slurp, slurp."

We both shiver
and hold hands.
My cousin doesn't like cats,
and I don't like moths.

Just then, something
flutters against the tent,
flapping its wings.
"*Meow, meow,*" it says.
We hug each other.
"*Meow, meow, slurp, slurp,*" it says.
We don't make a sound.

"Look, Simon," I say,
"just go away. You are not funny."
We lie still for a moment,
  ignoring him.
  Finally, I tell my cousin,
"That's nothing.
  Wait until you hear about
  the Tree Creeper."

"The Tree Creeper looks like a
stick insect that climbs
from tree to tree.
It hugs the branches,
waiting to drop down
on anyone walking below."

"Never pitch your tent
  under a tree," I warn her.
"If you do,
  the Tree Creeper
  will drop down
  in the middle of the night
  and crawl inside your tent.
  It will crush you
  in its stick-like arms.
  Crunch! Crunch!"

Neither one of us
likes this story.
We reach out
and hold hands.
I don't know where
I got such a horrible idea.

Suddenly, there is a *BANG!*
It sounds like a tree branch
has landed on top of the tent.

We hear, "Crunch, crunch, crunch."
We scream and hide our eyes.
Then, we hear a silly laugh.

"Simon, go away!" we yell.
"You spoil everything."
Now, my cousin
is very quiet.

I begin to think that
I might have won the game.
Then, she says to me,
"You don't know about
the Invisible Man, do you?"

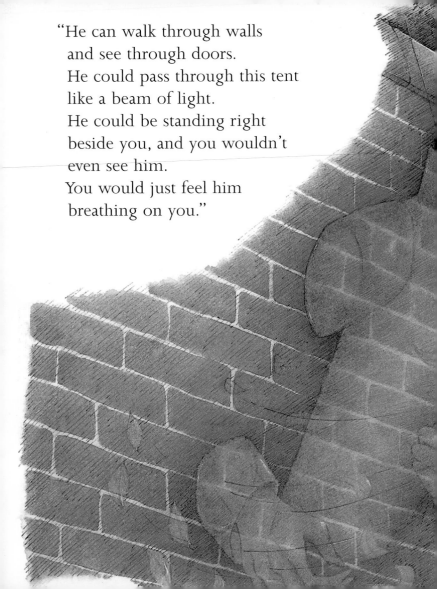

"He can walk through walls
  and see through doors.
  He could pass through this tent
  like a beam of light.
  He could be standing right
  beside you, and you wouldn't
  even see him.
  You would just feel him
  breathing on you."

"It doesn't matter where
you pitch your tent," she tells me.
"The Invisible Man will get you.
Nothing can keep him out."

Now, it is really dark outside.
There isn't a sound.
I am lying here,
wide awake,
thinking about this monster.
It may be coming
to get me right now,
and I won't even
be able to see it.

I grab my cousin's arm.
"What happens
  if he gets you?" I ask.
  She yawns.
"He dissolves you," she says,
"so you are invisible, too."
"And then what?" I ask.
  There is no answer.
"THEN WHAT HAPPENS?"

My cousin has gone to sleep.
I can hear her breathing deeply beside me.

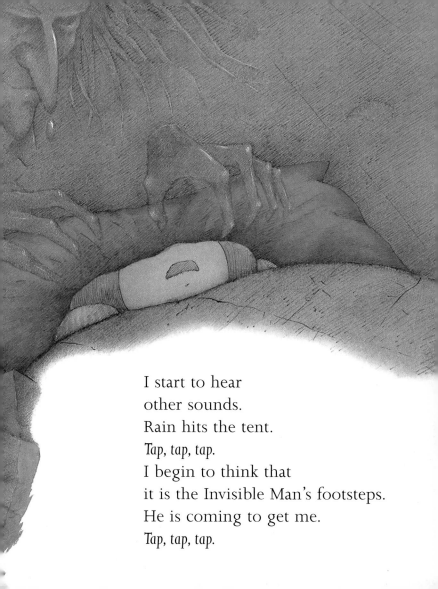

I start to hear
other sounds.
Rain hits the tent.
Tap, tap, tap.
I begin to think that
it is the Invisible Man's footsteps.
He is coming to get me.
Tap, tap, tap.

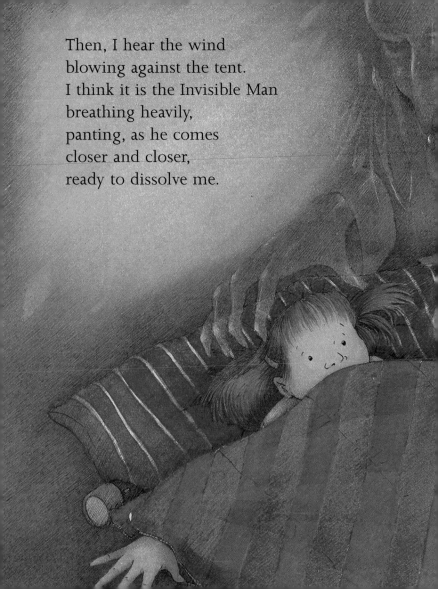

Then, I hear the wind
blowing against the tent.
I think it is the Invisible Man
breathing heavily,
panting, as he comes
closer and closer,
ready to dissolve me.

I slide down into my sleeping bag and hide.

Then, I hear a ripping sound.
Someone is trying to get in.

I reach for my flashlight.
I switch it on just in time
to see the tent flap
burst open and a horrible face
appear in the gap.

"Can I come in?" asks Simon.
"It's raining out here,
 and I'm getting wet."
I take a deep breath.
"Oh, Simon!" I say.
This time, I don't
 send him away.

He crouches down
between my cousin and me,
and we start to giggle.
Then, I remember the snacks
my cousin and I brought with us.
"Are you hungry?" I ask.
Simon grins.

We sit side by side,
just the two of us,
and eat our midnight feast.
We whisper quietly
so we won't wake up my cousin.
That would spoil everything.

In the morning,
if my cousin asks me
who ate her food,
I will tell her that
it must have been
the Invisible Man.